NINJA STRIKE

ADAM BLADE

ORCHARD

MEET TEAM HERO ...

JACK

POWER: Super-strength

LIKES: Ventura City FC

DISLIKES: Bullies

014268965 0

Special thanks to Tabitha Jones

ORCHARD BOOKS

First published in Great Britain in 2019 by The Watts Publishing Group

1 3 5 7 9 10 8 6 4 2

Text © 2019 Beast Quest Limited
Cover and inside illustrations by Dynamo
© Beast Quest Limited 2019

Team Hero is a registered trademark in the European Union
Series created by Beast Quest Limited, London

The moral rights of the author and illustrator have been asserted.
All characters and events in this publication, other than those clearly in the public domain,
are fictitious and any resemblance to real persons, living or dead, is purely coincidental.

All rights reserved.
No part of this publication may be reproduced, stored in a retrieval system, or transmitted, in any form
or by any means, without the prior permission in writing of the publisher, nor be otherwise circulated in
any form of binding or cover other than that in which it is published and without a similar condition
including this condition being imposed on the subsequent purchaser.

A CIP catalogue record for this book is available from the British Library.

ISBN 978 1 40835 558 9

Printed and bound by CPI Group (UK) Ltd, Croydon, CR0 4YY

The paper and board used in this book are made from wood from responsible sources.

Orchard Books
An imprint of Hachette Children's Group
Part of The Watts Publishing Group Limited
Carmelite House, 50 Victoria Embankment, London EC4Y 0DZ

An Hachette UK Company
www.hachette.co.uk
www.hachettechildrens.co.uk

RUBY

POWER: Fire vision
LIKES: Comic books
DISLIKES: Small spaces

DANNY

POWER: Super-hearing, able to generate son blasts
LIKES: Pizza

CONTENTS

PROLOGUE

THE AGENT leaned forward in his chair, craning over the shard of aquamarine metal in the centre of his desk. He rubbed his gauntleted hands together. A diffuse blue light shone down from the ceiling, making the compass fragment gleam. Using a slender glass pipette, he dispensed a single drop of shimmering Xanthrum liquid on to it. Immediately, the shard flared bright blue and spun to point due east. The Agent poked the compass piece gently — it veered off course, then snapped back to point east again. *Interesting* ... He pressed a button on his gauntlet. A projected 3D map shimmered into life before him. *Now, let's see where this compass piece is leading* ...

"Eh hem!" A female voice cut though his train of thought. He looked up at the slender, dark-skinned woman who was watching him, one eyebrow raised.

"Ah, Serenade," he said. He had almost forgotten her.

"I'm guessing you're not paying me to watch you tinker with that thing," she said. "What's the plan?"

Still pleased with his discovery, the Agent let her show of impatience pass. This time.

"It seems all three compass pieces are connected," he told her. "This fragment indicates the location of the next one. See here." The Agent pointed to the holo-map. "All the ancient Taah Lu sites are marked by green dots. This piece shows the way to the second part of the compass." He traced a line across the map with his finger, stopping at a glowing dot located deep within the jungle. He felt a flicker of unease. He had heard that this particular Taah Lu site was riddled with dangerous traps. *But that is why I hire underlings*, he thought, smiling.

The woman shrugged. "I can't imagine an ancient ruin giving me too much trouble."

"You'd be surprised," the Agent told her. "However, your special abilities coupled with your martial arts training will be useful in evading whatever dangers the site contains."

The Agent pressed another button on his wrist. A drawer opened

smoothly before him. He took out
a long, curved sword. "The blade of
this katana is nano-sharpened. It
will cut through almost anything," he
said, extending the weapon towards
the woman, who took the sword
and briefly mimed fighting invisible
opponents. It sliced through the air
with barely a whisper as Serenade
expertly tested it.

She smiled. "This will do nicely."

The Agent then took several small
metal globes from his drawer. At
the press of a button, they whirred
rapidly into life, zipping upwards to
hover in the air.

"These drones will aid you in the search of the ruin," he said. "Find the second compass piece and bring it to me. Eliminate anyone who gets in your way."

X MARKS THE SPOT

"THERE HAS to be something you can do to help her!" Ruby said, speaking to the flickering image of Professor Rufus projected above her mother's camp bed. Standing behind Ruby in the half darkness of the ruined jungle temple, Jack and Danny exchanged anxious glances. Even Jack could see Dr Jabari's condition was going downhill fast. Their enemy, the Agent, had poisoned her with a strange liquid metal called Xanthrum. Now, in the pale light filtering through tangled vines, Jack could see her skin and eyes had taken on a greyish tinge. Despite the jungle air being stiflingly hot, her whole body shivered and her skin felt cold to the touch.

Dr Jabari's eyes flickered open and she lifted a hand as if to calm her daughter. Even that effort seemed too much for her. She quickly let her hand fall, her eyes rolling closed.

"Please!" Ruby begged Rufus,

wringing her hands.

Professor Rufus shook his head, his freckled face lined with sorrow. "The data your Oracles have sent us regarding this metal doesn't fit with anything we know," he said. "In fact, it makes no sense at all. Our only hope of finding a cure is to locate the Agent. If we had a pure sample of the metal or if—" The communication channel crackled suddenly and zigzag lines distorted Rufus's face. A moment later, his image vanished, leaving them staring at a crumbling wall.

Ruby let out a gasp of distress. Danny rested his hand on her shoulder. "Don't worry," he said. "Professor Yokata will get the link back up and running."

I hope so, Jack thought. After the Agent attacked the dig site at the Taah Lu temple, it hadn't been easy for Yokata  to restore communications with Hero Academy. The link clearly still needed work.

Ruby turned, her orange eyes flashing. "How can I not worry, when Mum ..." Ruby's voice faltered, but then she met his eyes, her jaw set. "Rufus said that we need to find the Agent. So, let's go. Now!"

Jack nodded. "We'll do whatever it takes," he said, "but we need a plan first. The jungle's huge, and we don't even know where to start." Ruby's shoulders sagged. At the look of defeat in her eyes, Jack felt a rush of frustration and sympathy.

There must be a way to find the Agent!

He scanned the dim, ruined temple

while he wracked his brains. Professor Yokata crouched by the battered comms link apparatus, screwdriver in hand. Madison and Simon, the two other Team Hero students on the mission, sat in a corner sorting through what remained of their supplies. Bent together over a table, two of Dr Jabari's archaeology team examined artefacts uncovered from beneath the temple.

Jack thought of the engraved stone tablet the team had discovered earlier in the dig — it had a strange blue metal fragment hidden inside it. The fragment was part of a compass that would show the location of an ancient, deadly weapon. The Agent had that fragment now, but he needed two more …

That's it! Jack thought. "Maybe we don't know where the Agent is," he said, "but we do know that he's looking for the next compass fragment." He touched his earpiece, speaking to his Oracle device. "Hawk, can you bring up an image of the carving that hid the compass fragment?"

"Certainly," Hawk's tinny voice replied in his ear.

A holographic image of the stone

tablet appeared before them. The three friends peered closely at the geometric symbols and pictograms etched into the stone. They had seen the hologram before and believed the bottom part of the tablet depicted a battle between two races: one human, and the other a group of strangely tall beings who wore pointed helmets and had six fingers on each hand. Dr Jabari had managed to decipher the strange writing-like symbols too. They explained that three compass shards had been hidden at sacred sites across the jungle. Each piece could be used to locate the next. Once assembled, the compass would point to the weapon. The Agent had recovered the first fragment by destroying the stone tablet in which it had been hidden.

The only part of the stone tablet's inscription left unexplained was a snaking line running across the centre. Three dots had been engraved at seemingly random intervals along its length. But the more Jack looked at the squiggly line, the more it seemed familiar ...

"Look!" he said. "The shape of the line looks just like the Parra River! Hawk, can you overlay a map of the jungle on to the tablet?" he asked his Oracle. A heartbeat later, a second hologram overlapped the first.

"A perfect match!" Danny cried.

Ruby's expression brightened, and she pointed at something on the map. "The first dot is located here, at this temple."

"And since the first compass piece was hidden here," said Danny, "it would make sense for the other dots to show the locations of the final two pieces."

"It's definitely worth a try!" a firm voice said from behind them. Jack turned to see Professor Yokata gazing at the map. She looked weary, her short hair spiky with sweat, but a hint of a smile softened her stern face. "Good work!" she said. "Unfortunately, I haven't been able to salvage enough of *Arrow III* to get the craft flying again — but I did find the hoverboards we had stowed. You three go and investigate the closest site for any sign of the Agent. Simon and Madison can check out the other one. I'll stay here and attend to Dr Jabari. Send word if you need backup."

● ● ●

Jack leaned into the breeze, shifting his bodyweight to steer his hoverboard between the closely

packed trees. Ruby sped through the
jungle ahead.

"Hey! We won't get there any faster
if I have to scrape you off a tree,"
Danny called, bringing up the rear.
Glossy leaves and bright flowers
rushed by on either side, and vines

dangled from above. Through the blur of vegetation, Jack caught glimpses of the Parra River, wide and sluggish, green with silt. Birds and monkeys let out trills and hoots of alarm as they passed. Before long, Jack noticed a low, rumbling roar that grew louder the further they travelled, rising to a pounding flood of sound that drowned out everything else.

Water?

"You are now approaching your final destination," Hawk suddenly chanted in Jack's ear. Ahead, Ruby passed through a curtain of hanging vines and stopped abruptly. Jack ducked beneath the leafy tendrils after her, and gasped. Danny let out a whistle. The Parra River spilled before them into a wide, choppy lake. On the far side, the tallest waterfall Jack had ever seen loomed into the sky, a furious white torrent crashing over rocks, sending out clouds of rainbow spray over the lake. The cliff disappeared into the jungle on either side, blocking their way.

Jack ran his eyes up the waterfall. He spied what looked like a cave mouth, just visible through the curtain of water about halfway up the cliff face.

"Now I think we have to climb," Jack said, leading his friends over the lake towards the waterfall, their hoverboards skimming the choppy water. As they neared the falls, the roar became almost deafening and fine spray soaked Jack's skin. He swerved towards the rocky shore.

When he reached firm ground, he powered down his hoverboard and hopped off. Ruby and Danny followed suit.

Jack felt a wave of vertigo as he started to climb up the craggy cliff face, slick with spray from the tumbling falls. Wedging his fingers and toes in crevices in the slippery rock, he hauled himself upwards. Water crashed past in a dizzying rush making his ears ring and his head whirl. Even the rock beneath his scaled hands seemed to throb with the violence of the falls.

Before long, the lake below looked no bigger than a village pond, and Jack's arms burned from the climb. Finally, he reached an overhang that sheltered the cave from the falls, and a shallow ledge led towards the cave mouth. Jack pulled himself up on to the narrow platform and started shuffling sideways.

Danny went next, pressing himself against the cliff. "Look out!" Ruby cried. Nerves thrumming, Jack glanced towards the cave mouth to see a fist-sized metal drone flit from the darkness towards him, a red light flashing at its centre, spurting a blue metallic liquid towards him.

Xanthrum! If it hits me I'm dead!

CHAPTER 2

DRONE ATTACK

JACK PIVOTED as best he could on the narrow ledge. His back hit rock, and he pressed himself into it.

SPLAT! The Xanthrum hit right where he'd been standing, dissolving the rockface into a smoking, oozing mess. He realised with a jolt of shock that the Agent had more than one type of Xanthrum. *This one's a deadly acid!* The hovering drone darted towards him, ready to shoot again.

FZZZZ! Twin beams of orange fire shot from Ruby's eyes, hitting the strange orb. It crackled and spat sparks, then dropped like a stone. But two more drones sped out from the darkness of the cave.

Ruby fired a second blast, and Danny let rip a terrific roar of a sonic blast, making Jack wince. The drones zigzagged out of reach, then arced back around, coming in for another attack.

A bright jet of blue-tinged metal

spurted from one, shooting towards
Danny.

"Climb!" Jack cried. Danny leapt,
scrambling up on to a tiny lip of stone
just as the liquid metal struck the
rock. The brittle ledge sizzled and
fizzed, then crumbled, taking Danny
down with it.

"Help!" Danny cried, wide-eyed with
terror.

Jack shot out a hand and grabbed
his friend's wrist but, as he jerked to
a stop, Danny's head knocked against
the rockface. With the super strength
of his scaled hand, Jack heaved him
up. Danny clambered shakily on to

the platform beside him, a red bruise swelling on his cheek.

Fzzzzz! Ruby aimed her flame vision at the drones again, but they zipped away. She turned her head, sending out two more searing beams.

Crack! One of the silver balls plummeted, trailing flames from Ruby's strike. The other turned its flashing red eye on her and fired.

"To me!" Jack cried. He shoved Danny behind him towards the cave, and held out a hand for Ruby. Ruby leapt over the crumbling rock ledge and Jack pulled her clear just as the corrosive liquid metal struck where she'd been standing, sending up clouds of acrid smoke. The remaining silver drone whizzed in close, its red eye flashing. Jack dodged the drone then opened his hand and swatted the orb like a fly. With a satisfying *clunk*, it bounced away down the

cliff, crackling with red light, and disappeared into the foaming water.

Danny let out a shaky laugh. "That was way too close," he said, rubbing at one of his outsized bat-like ears. Blood smeared his hand when he pulled it away.

"Are you all right?" Ruby asked him.

"I'll live," Danny said. Then he winced. "But I think Owl took a hit when I fell. He's babbling machine code. Loudly!" Danny tapped behind his ear to turn off his Oracle's sound. "That's better!" he said.

"Then let's go," Ruby said, her eyes suddenly fierce. "Those drones definitely looked like the Agent's tech, so we're on the right track!"

Jack followed Ruby beneath the falls, towards a strange pile of rubble at the cave mouth. He bent down to inspect it. He picked up a chunk of smoothly cut stone.

"Look," he said, pointing to the rectangular entrance to the cave. "It looks like there was a door here, but something chopped it to pieces."

"Maybe those drones?" Ruby said. "That blue metal they shoot dissolves rock."

"Possibly," Jack said. "But the cuts are too regular, and there's no residue. We'll need to keep our eyes peeled for more than just drones inside there."

"And our ears," Danny said, grinning and tucking his shaggy black hair back out of the way.

Jack crunched over the pile of broken stone and peered into the dark entrance. "Hawk, engage night vision," he said. A visor slid down to cover Jack's eyes. Immediately, he could see a wide square tunnel outlined in shades of green leading steadily downwards.

"Sorry, guys," Danny said from behind him. He tapped at his

malfunctioning Oracle. "My night vision's not working."

"Let's try torchlight," Jack suggested. The three friends switched modes, their silvery rays glancing off carvings of strange faces and simplified animal shapes cut into the tunnel walls.

"This is another Taah Lu site of some sort," Ruby said. "Mum would be so excited to see this ..." Jack heard a catch in her voice.

"We'll find the Agent," he said. "Your mum will be setting up a dig here in no time."

They trudged on, gradually leaving

the roar of the waterfall behind them.
Their bobbing torches cast eerie
shadows over the carved walls. In the
still, charged silence, Jack felt the
hair on the back of his neck prickle.
He found himself glancing over his
shoulder, listening for the sound of
breathing or footsteps that didn't
belong to them.

Ahead, a doorway gaped darkly
on one side of the passage. As they
reached it a blast of cold, musty air
rushed out, making Jack shiver. He
peered through to find a winding
stairway leading downwards. Ahead,
more doorways opened on to narrower

passages and staircases, all leading
deeper underground.

"Hawk, can you map these tunnels?"
Jack asked his Oracle.

*"The stone is too thick for accurate
measurements,"* Hawk answered after

a pause. *"However, I can detect many levels below this one."*

Their footsteps rang in the cool, still air as they travelled steadily deeper. A damp, earthy smell rose from the stone. Jack stared into the darkness beyond the reach of their light beams, his nerves thrumming.

Suddenly Danny spun. "I hear something," he hissed. Jack and Ruby stopped to listen. Jack heard a faint scrape, followed by a whisper of laughter.

"I don't think we're alone down here," Ruby said.

Jack drew Blaze as Danny unhooked

his energy crossbow from his back. They crept onwards. Jack and Danny readied their weapons. But then a scuffle of footsteps came from behind them, along with the same dry laugh as before. Jack whipped around but saw only his own wavering shadow. They shuffled silently along the passage, hearing the ghost of laughter at times, but seeing nothing.

Finally, the tunnel opened abruptly into a vast chamber. Jack ran the beam of his torch around the massive room. The light glanced off towering square pillars of stone, blocky altar-like structures and, in the far distance, the rectangular openings of dozens more carved tunnels.

"This place is huge!" Ruby said. "It looks like way more than just a temple. It must be a whole underground city."

"Oh, it's a city, all right," a female voice said from behind them.

They all spun, their torches converging on the slender form of a tall woman wearing a close-fitting bodysuit decorated with silver bands. Her long black hair was pulled back in a high ponytail. Her teeth and the whites of her eyes stood out brightly in the torchlight as she smiled at them, catlike.

"A dead city," she said, drawing a katana blade from her belt and falling into a practised fighting stance. "A fitting place to die, don't you think?"

CHAPTER 3

KATANA STRIKE

"WHO ARE you?" Jack asked, sinking into a crouch, ready to meet any attack. Before the slender woman could answer, Ruby stormed forward, fists raised, her orange eyes burning like coals.

"Where's the Agent?" she cried. "Tell me now, or you're toast!"

"Well, aren't you brave?" the woman said, smiling. "My name's Serenade. I'm also called the Silent Shadow." Suddenly, her sword arm flashed out so fast Jack barely saw it move. Ruby leapt back with a yelp, holding her shoulder. Blood welled beneath her fingers.

Ruby gaped at the woman, then gritted her teeth. "You asked for it!"

FZZZZ! Bright fire-beams sizzled from her eyes, lighting up the cave. Serenade moved so fast, her blurred form merged with the flickering shadows. Ruby's flames left scorch marks on the walls and pillars.

A dry chuckle from behind him made Jack turn. Their opponent stood, hand on hip, leaning against an altar towards the far left of the room. *How did she move so fast? She must have super-ability!*

"Oh dear, you'll never catch me like that," Serenade said.

Ruby sent two more crackling beams towards Serenade. The woman vanished into a fuzzy haze of glinting speed.

"Ow!" Ruby cried, and spun, holding the base of her spine as if something had jabbed her. Jack turned too, to find Serenade swinging her katana at

his chest. He leapt back, lifting Blaze
to swipe the woman's weapon aside,

 but Serenade whipped
it out of reach, then
lunged. Jack darted
aside, and Danny
fired an energy bolt
from his crossbow.
Once again, Serenade
almost seemed to
disappear, only the
blurred trail of the
silver bands on her
suit suggesting her movements.

CRASH! A bolt from Danny's energy
crossbow smashed into the wall.

Now Serenade was standing in the centre of the vast room. "I have to admit, I expected at least a bit of a fight."

Ruby's eyes flared with flame and Danny howled a sonic blast at once. With breathtaking speed, Serenade flipped and cartwheeled out of the way. In the confusion of torchlight and flames, Jack lost sight of Serenade once again. *This is hopeless!*

Suddenly, pain exploded in Jack's sword arm as something struck him, and a second later his legs were swept away. Ruby fell on top of him and Danny sprawled down beside them, clutching his stomach.

Jack untangled himself from Ruby and struggled to his feet to see Serenade come to a stop on top of a long, low stone structure near the back wall of the room. His friends pulled themselves up beside him.

Serenade sighed. "When the Agent tracked me down, I wasn't sure it was worth my effort joining him," she said, casually balancing her katana on the tip of one finger. "But then he offered me this special combat suit, and this nano-sharpened katana, plus a handsome payment, all for a little bit of help finding an ancient artefact.

Well ... I thought it might be a fun challenge." She twirled the katana so fast, the blade was almost invisible. "But the Agent said I'd be facing Heroes, not children with torches strapped to their heads bumbling about in the dark. How disappointing." As Serenade spoke, Jack noticed part of the ceiling had collapsed behind her, blocking a handful of exits from the room. He caught Ruby's eye, then Danny's, and gestured towards the rubble.

"Surround her," he mouthed. Danny nodded, then slipped to the right. Jack crept left, while Ruby edged forwards, heading straight for the woman.

Serenade barely bothered to look up as they approached. Instead, she lazily traced the tip of her katana over the lines of a mosaic at her feet. "I'd be careful in here if I were you," she said. "I've heard the place is full of surprises ... Still, it should be simple enough to find the compass fragment, even with all the booby traps the Taah Lu set." Serenade flipped her blade upwards, sending it spinning towards the cavern roof.

Ruby growled. "Why don't you stop showing off and tell us where the Agent is?"

Serenade snatched her katana from the air and leaned towards them, her eyes flashing. "And why would I do that?" she asked. "If you want something from me, you'll have to take it."

"If you say so!" said Jack. He sprinted from the side, brandishing Blaze as Danny charged in from the opposite direction and Ruby ran straight towards Serenade, turning her head from side to side, scorching the air with long, arcing beams of fire.

The flames reflected in Serenade's eyes as she calmly watched them approach. But with piles of collapsed brickwork right behind her, and with Jack and Danny closing in from either side, she was cornered.

"You're trapped, now drop your weapon," Jack said, keeping his stance low and wide, ready to leap into action if the woman moved.

"I really do commend your effort," Serenade said. "Unfortunately, you're the ones who are actually trapped." Her lips twisted into a wry smile, and she brought her boot down, stamping hard on the centre of the mosaic before her. "Goodbye!"

A hideous grating groan shuddered through the chamber, and a juddering

vibration ran up through Jack's body.
Oh no! His heart lurched as the entire
swath of floor beneath him gave way.
Danny let out a panicked cry and
Ruby screamed as they slid all down
a wide, almost vertical chute, falling
into darkness.

CHAPTER 4

A DEADLY PUZZLE

JACK'S KNEES almost buckled as
he landed at the bottom of the stone
chute. Ruby dropped lightly to her
feet beside him. Danny tumbled to the
ground, rolled over and scrambled up,
covered in dust. Jack glanced about.
They had arrived in a long, narrow,
corridor-like room with only one door,

right at the far end. A complex mosaic patterned the floor, and when Jack turned his torch on, it illuminated hundreds of thin, web-like threads running from wall to wall.

"That was some ride!" Danny said, stepping back and grinning at his friends.

"Wait!" Jack cried, but he was too late – Danny backed right into one of the silvery strands, snapping it in half. A clanking rattle and a loud grating sound echoed through the room. Danny's eyes went wide with fear, and Jack felt his insides turn to liquid as the chamber walls inched closer together, then jolted to a stop. Danny stood frozen, barely breathing, then quickly stepped back to Jack's side.

"So, we should not break the tripwires," Ruby said, her voice low as she ran her torch over the dense network of strands. "I think we can manage that."

Jack nodded, though being both taller and broader than Ruby, he didn't feel quite so sure. He stepped forward, ducking beneath the first strand. Two more parallel wires crossed his path, just centimetres away. He rotated and lifted his leg high over the first strand, and posted himself sideways through the gap. He gently lifted his back leg over, then let out a shuddering breath as he glanced back to see Ruby and Danny watching him. He'd come only half a metre, and already his bodysuit stuck to him, damp with sweat. He still had at least thirty metres to go. *This is going to be tough ...* Ruby slipped beneath the first strand, and Danny ducked, quickly joining her. Jack started to ease himself through a narrow triangular gap between three wires, then froze, momentarily blinded as Ruby and Danny each bent, accidentally sending their torch beams into his face.

"I think we'll need to move one at a time," Jack said. "Otherwise we won't be able to see these wires."

He shuffled towards the next gossamer-thin thread and felt the tile beneath his foot shift, then settle with a loud click.

That didn't sound good …

Jack stood frozen, his heart in his mouth, wondering if the floor was about to open beneath him again, or if …

Whoosh!

He looked up to see a massive ball of

rock falling towards him. He flung up his arms, catching the huge sphere in his scaled hands. *Phew! Without my strength, that would have smashed my skull.* Jack let out a shaky breath

and set the ball gently on the floor at his feet.

"OK, so we can't tread on those either," Danny said, pointing at the black star-shaped tile Jack had triggered. "I wonder if we can tread on any of the others ..." Danny frowned, gazing over the coloured stars and squares all over the floor. "Hmm." He gingerly put out a foot and pressed his toe down on a red square.

Whoomph! Another ball plummeted straight towards Danny's head. Jack dived back the way he'd come, arms outstretched as he cannoned into Danny, throwing him sideways and snatching the deadly weight of rock from the air. The tripwires Jack had carefully avoided now snapped all around him. The clanking, groaning walls slowly dragged inwards. Jack hit the ground, losing his grip on the ball, which rolled away and severed more strands, while Danny broke at least half a dozen more as he struggled to stand up.

"Run!" Ruby screamed, as the walls on either side cranked closer. Jack took in the rapidly narrowing space, the distance they still had left to go, and nodded. *It's our only hope.*

"Go!" he cried. "I'll bring up the rear!"

Ruby sprinted away, Danny right behind her. Jack bolted after them, the whole room shaking around him. He could see the walls closing on Ruby and Danny ahead. A mighty stone thudded to the ground, right between them and Jack. With no space to dodge around it, Jack leapt, hearing another rock crash down behind him as he landed and kept running. Fear jolted through him as he realised the walls were so close he could reach out and touch them. He kept his eyes on the exit ahead and raced on.

"Nearly there!" Ruby cried. But with

more strands breaking with every step, the walls jerked together faster than ever. Danny stumbled and fell, then picked himself up, scrambling after Ruby.

We'll never make it out, Jack realised. *Unless ...* He threw his arms out to either side of him, bracing his body between the walls. A hideous screeching sound filled the narrow space as the walls ground to a halt. Ruby sped on, leaping a red tile, then throwing herself through the exit. Danny careened after her. Both safe, they turned and beckoned frantically to Jack.

Sweat dripped into Jack's eyes and his muscles trembled as the strain on his arms became almost unbearable. He took a deep breath, steadying his thundering heartbeat. *I've practised this move!* he told himself. *I can do this!* Then he let go of the walls and threw himself into a front flip, pushing off the ground with the super-strength of his scaled hands. His body arched high into the air and the room sped by in a blur. *Thud!* Jack landed on his feet.

BOOM! The walls slammed together behind him so hard he felt the sound rumble in his chest and debris rattled down from the ceiling.

"You did it!" Danny said, clapping Jack on the back.

Jack nodded, struggling to get his breath. "Only just!"

"Well, that's much better than 'not quite'!" Ruby said. "But which way should we go now?" They had arrived in yet another passage that sloped away into darkness. Corridors branched off on either side, but glancing through the first few, Jack saw they also all appeared to lead down.

"How can every turn keep taking us lower?" he said. "We must be practically at the centre of the earth by now."

"We are not quite that deep," Hawk said in his ear. *"But I do detect we are significantly below sea level."*

"Well, I guess we just keep going," Danny said. "After all, we can't exactly go back the way we came."

Jack rested his hand on Blaze's hilt and Danny kept his crossbow raised as they followed the seemingly endless passage. They moved softly, scanning the way ahead with their torches for any sign of Serenade. As they passed a doorway, something shiny caught Jack's eye ... something metallic in the darkness beyond the door.

He signalled for his friends to stop, and put a finger to his lips as he drew Blaze. Danny trained his crossbow on the doorway and Ruby watched closely, her orange eyes glimmering. Jack peeked inside. What he saw took his breath away. The room looked like some sort of armoury, or a warehouse, but he couldn't make sense of the contents. He stepped through the doorway and beckoned his friends to follow. Gleaming piles of gold-coloured cogs, scythe-like blades and curved metal plates covered the floor. All looked polished and new, but Jack knew they had to be ancient.

"Look!" Ruby said, pointing to a set of pictograms etched on the wall along with strange geometric markings. "I can read some of this. Mum showed me how." She put out a hand and traced a complex symbol. "This one means 'soldier'," she said. "And this means 'weapon' ..." Then she gasped. "I think these are the parts needed to make some sort of mechanical soldier."

"Hmm. It doesn't look much like a soldier to me," Danny said, frowning at the shining piles of metal. Jack stepped past Ruby, heading further into the room. He ran his torch over more of the wall, revealing part of a sprawling carved mural. The carving seemed to depict a legion of Taah Lu warriors armed with spears and swords. A huge metal ball covered in blades bore down on the army, and in its wake, Jack could see a trail of fallen men and women.

"Look at this," he said.

Danny came to his side. "OK ... I guess I can see how that thing might be dangerous. But still, I reckon Team Hero could take it out."

Ruby pressed further into the room

then let out a whistle. "Could we take out a whole army of them?" Jack and Danny joined her to see a carving of what appeared to be thousands of the spherical metal soldiers. A city with towers and spires had been etched into the rock too, but all the buildings looked half demolished, smoke billowing into the sky. They stood in silence, taking it in.

"That looks a lot like Chancellor Rex's vision of the future," Ruby said eventually, her voice sounding small.

"You're right," Jack said, remembering the burning city Rex had shown them, overrun by slicing

blades. He turned to look at all the
gleaming metal parts stacked in the
room behind them. He shuddered.

"The Agent isn't just after one weapon ... he's planning to wake an entire army!"

CHAPTER 5

A HIDDEN ARMY

AS JACK led his friends onwards through the underground city, dread coiled in his stomach as he imagined the carnage a whole army of these strange mechanical soldiers could unleash — all the innocent people who would suffer. *But the Agent needs all three compass pieces to find the rest of the army ...* he told himself. *We still have time to stop him.*

"Wait! I hear something!" Danny hissed. He turned his head, backed up a bit then rounded a corner. Jack and Ruby followed him through a warren of passages, down a worn stairway and on to another level. Here, Jack could make out the steady drip of water and what sounded like muffled voices coming from ahead.

The heroes rounded a corner to find dim blue light spilling from a stone archway at the far end. Jack heard the cool, reasoned tones of Serenade's voice, but couldn't make out her words.

"Better turn off our torches so the light doesn't give us away," Jack whispered. They all crept silently forwards. Jack reached the archway and looked through, seeing it open on to a high mezzanine floor about halfway up the side of an enormous cylindrical chamber. He felt awed by the building skills of the ancient Taah Lu.

Blue orbs suspended in the air cast a soft glow throughout the arena-like space. *Those look like the Agent's tech*, Jack thought. The hovering lights revealed slender bridges and majestic flights of stairs connecting more mezzanine floors and balconies. A high domed ceiling arched overhead, almost lost in shadow, and carvings decorated the walls. But the room had seen better days. A great crack ran across the ceiling, and water dripped through, trickling down into the flooded depths of the bottom few floors. The still, inky pool created by the dripping reflected the pale lights above.

Jack noticed a shimmering gleam coming from an alcove on the far side of the chamber. Serenade stood just inside with her back to them, facing a projected holo-screen. A narrow

stone bridge spanned the cylindrical space, leading directly towards her. But Jack knew going that way would leave them too exposed. Instead, he led Ruby and Danny around the mezzanine, keeping to the shadows. They stopped behind a huge column close to Serenade's alcove and peered out.

"Yes, but as I said, there's a catch ..." Serenade was speaking to a projected hologram of the Agent's masked face. "It's underneath about fifteen metres of water."

"So?" the Agent said. "I presume you can swim to it?"

"Not without my eardrums exploding, no," Serenade snapped.

"Well, I suppose I'll just have to fetch the fragment myself!" the Agent said. "This will be reflected in your payment. Send a drone back to show me the way. And don't go anywhere! I expect you to protect the shard when I arrive."

Serenade shrugged. "So long as that's also reflected in my payment," she said. The hologram flickered and vanished. Jack ducked back out of sight. He turned to see Ruby's eyes glowing.

"The Agent's coming," she said. "We'll be able to capture him and find a cure for my mum."

Jack nodded. "But we'll have a better chance if we take out Serenade first."

"Agreed," Danny said. Then he flashed Jack and Ruby a broad smile. "Sounds like time for a bit of teamwork!"

"How about a pincer manoeuvre?" Jack asked. "If I can lure her on to the bridge, do you think you two could keep her there?"

Ruby grinned, a flash of fire lighting up her amber eyes. "I think we could manage that," she said. "I'll take the far end. Danny, you wait this side. Let's go."

Lifting Blaze, Jack edged towards Serenade's alcove. Ruby crept in the opposite direction, heading towards the far end of the narrow bridge, while Danny stayed hidden, his crossbow raised and ready.

As Jack reached the alcove, Serenade turned.

"You again," she said, rolling her eyes. "I thought I'd seen the last of you. But I suppose killing you will give me something to do while I wait for the Agent!" Then, in a blur of super-fast movement, she closed the distance between them and slashed her katana towards Jack's gut. He leapt back,

barely escaping the first blow before
Serenade was aiming a second one
at him. Somehow, he knocked her
blade aside, backing up on to the
bridge. Serenade prowled after him,
her dark eyes filled with amusement
as she rained down lightning-fast
strikes. As he blocked and parried
the relentless barrage, Jack risked a
quick glance over his shoulder, seeing
Ruby creeping through the shadows,
moving into place at the far end of the
bridge. Blaze's pommel felt slippery
with sweat and Jack's arm muscles
burned with exhaustion as he carried
on fighting, straining all his senses to

keep up with Serenade's super-speed.

Behind Serenade, Danny slipped into view at the near end of the bridge, crossbow raised. *If I can hold on just a bit longer, this might actually work!* Jack deflected another barely visible katana swipe.

Serenade paused for a moment, smiling. "Had enough yet?" she asked, swishing her blade through the air in a shimmering arc. Instead of parrying, Jack sidestepped — right off the ledge of the bridge.

"Freeze!" Ruby shouted, as Jack grabbed the stone lip of the bridge and hung there, dangling by one hand. *Now Ruby and Danny both have a clear line of fire!*

"You're trapped," Danny cried from his end of the bridge.

Serenade let out a short growl of frustration.

Far below him, beneath the inky water, Jack noticed a blue-green gleam. His pulse quickened. "Hawk, zoom in on that glow!" he hissed to his Oracle. His visor dropped over his eyes, and now he could see three submerged statues. The tallest, a woman in flowing robes, had a glowing compass fragment hanging from a chain around its neck. *There it is ... But I couldn't make that swim without diving gear.*

Jack shoved Blaze through his belt, then swung hand over hand towards Danny and pulled himself up to stand behind his friend. Serenade crouched at the centre of the narrow walkway, glancing backwards and forwards between the heroes, her katana raised. The laser sight from Danny's crossbow marked a red dot on Serenade's chest, and Ruby kept her orange eyes fixed on the woman, blocking her escape.

"Put down your weapon, or we'll fire!" Ruby said. Serenade let out an irritated huff, then slowly lowered her katana on to the bridge.

"I don't need a weapon to beat you three," she said, looking first at Ruby, then turning her cool gaze on Danny and Jack. "Compared to mine, your powers are pathetic."

Ruby shrugged. "I don't know, I'd say they're coming in pretty handy right now." But then a familiar whooshing sound echoed up from below, and Jack felt a surge of dread.

"Not as handy as jet boots!" the Agent's mechanical voice boomed. The villain shot upwards to hover beside Serenade, thrusters firing from his booted feet and gleaming grenades clasped in each hand.

CHAPTER 6

SUNKEN TREASURE

JACK AND Danny both leapt off the
bridge as the Agent lobbed a Xanthrum
grenade. Its strange, noiseless explosion
sent up a storm of stone and a cloud of
smoke. Stinging acid metal spattered
against Jack's suit, searing holes in
the material. When the smoke cleared
Jack saw that most of the bridge was

gone. The Agent hovered above the inky water, holding a furious-looking Serenade by the scruff of her suit. He set her down on a flight of stairs then surged upwards, ejecting drones from compartments in his metal armour. From the far side of the room, Ruby sent a stream of flames towards him, but the Agent dodged them almost effortlessly, then tossed a grenade her way. Ruby threw herself into a dive, rolling away from the blast, then jumped to her feet.

"I'm not letting you get away after what you did to my mum!" she cried. "Give me the cure, now!" She raced towards a flight of stairs and started climbing, heading closer to where the Agent hovered.

A spherical drone zoomed towards Jack, red eye flashing. Danny aimed his crossbow and fired. The drone zipped sideways, and Danny's bolt whizzed across the room, hitting the wall. Chunks of rock clattered down, blocking a stairwell below. A spurt of metal shot towards Jack and he threw himself out of range. *SPLAT!* Blue Xanthrum hit the ground and fizzed away, boring right through the stone and revealing the mezzanine below. Jack heard a low groan echo down from the domed ceiling, followed by a crack. The floor trembled.

"I would avoid further compromising the structural integrity of this room if I were you," Hawk said in his ear.

"I'll deal with the girl," the Agent shouted down to Serenade. "You kill the other two! I want no one left to get in my way when I wake my army." Jack looked up to see Serenade whirl into a blur of movement.

"Engage ear defenders!" Danny called. Jack and Ruby tapped at their Oracles and then Danny let out a high-pitched burst of sound. Serenade rematerialised suddenly on her knees on a bridge

nearby, her hands clamped over her ears. Danny strode towards her, his sonic blast keeping her pinned to the ground.

Jack caught a flicker of movement from the corner of his eye and spun to see a drone racing his way. A jet of blue metal spurted towards his face. Terror swept through him and Jack hurled himself out of its path. He scrambled up to see the corrosive metal burn through the edge of the mezzanine and drip down into the pool below. Hissing clouds of vapour erupted skywards. A blue shimmer lit the inky water, and Jack looked down to see the acidic Xanthrum boring a hole right through the room's submerged stone floor. Clouds of bubbles erupted upwards. *That's how to get the compass piece!* Jack realised.

"Buy me some time," he shouted to his friends over the blare of Danny's sonic attack. "I've got an idea!"

He glanced up to see Ruby shooting fireballs at the Agent, who zoomed upwards to dodge the blasts, then flung a grenade. Ruby's flames vaporised it before it could hit her.

Serenade was still crouching under the onslaught of Danny's sonic blast, though the chamber walls had started to shake in time with the pulsing resonance of the sound. Sizzles and cracks rang out from above where Ruby and the Agent fought. *This place can't hold up for much longer*, Jack realised. But he pushed that thought aside, and ran down a twisting flight of stairs to the next mezzanine. Drones swarmed after him as he sped into the centre of a stone bridge, then turned.

A red eye dead ahead of him flashed, shooting out a spurt of liquid metal. Jack ducked. The Xanthrum sailed over his head, hitting the water with a bubbling hiss. Another blast of acidic metal arced towards him, and he leapt aside. With a terrific fizz, more steam erupted from below.

Jack's heart hammered as two more jets of Xanthrum surged towards him at once, aiming low. He turned and threw himself into a front flip, launching off the bridge towards the

mezzanine. He landed in a crouch and turned to see the bridge crumble into the water, melted rock and oozing metal plunging into the inky depths along with chunks of rubble.

Huge bubbles rose up from the shadowy depths where the acidic liquid metal had collected, burning through the bottom of the pool. The water started draining away, circling round and round as if a giant plug had been pulled.

"Danny, this way!" Jack shouted. Danny abruptly stopped his high-pitched sonic attack on Serenade. Jack watched as Serenade collapsed on to the bridge, moaning and clutching her ears.

Danny raced down the stairs towards Jack. Already, the head of the tallest statue peeked from above the surface, revealing the aquamarine compass shard around its neck. "I'm going to throw you to the statue to get the shard," Jack told him. "We need to make sure the Agent doesn't get it first."

Danny's face paled, but he let out a sigh and nodded. "Fine!" he said.

Jack cradled Danny's foot in his super-strong hands and launched him across the churning water to the top of the statue. As Danny threw his arms around the stone woman's neck, a terrific groan echoed through the chamber. With a sickening lurch of horror, Jack watched as half of the room's floor collapsed, and all the water

drained away at once. Danny tugged
the compass piece from the chain
around the statue's throat, then turned
to Jack, eyes shining. "I've got it!"

"No, you haven't!" the Agent shouted
from above. Jack looked up to see the
Agent zoom away from Ruby, rocket

boots firing, his dark eyes on Danny. But before the Agent could get far, the room shuddered. Cracks and booms echoed all around, and huge chunks of stone tumbled from the ceiling.

Serenade let out a cry and Jack looked over to see her holding an open gash on her thigh where a piece of masonry had hit her. She stumbled to her feet and hobbled from the bridge, heading towards an exit. The Agent beat her to it, zipping into the tunnel beyond. Serenade ducked through the archway behind him, and the Agent lobbed a grenade, collapsing the tunnel roof and blocking the way.

"It would appear that the structural integrity of—" Hawk started, but Jack cut him off.

"We have to get out of here!" he shouted to his friends as rubble crashed to the ground all around him.

Danny shoved the compass piece into his pocket and started climbing hand over hand down the side of the statue. Ruby was already speeding down a flight of stairs above, half stumbling as the chamber rocked and juddered.

Jack picked his way out over broken rock and fallen rubble towards the three huge statues just as Danny reached the floor. A terrific boom shuddered around them, rocking Jack on his feet as more masonry thundered to the ground. Ruby arrived beside them, breathing hard. "We have to go, now!" she cried pointing through the gaping hole in the ground towards a dark passage below.

How deep does this city go?

"Torch, please, Hawk," Jack said to his Oracle. He splashed through the gap to find a passageway choked with fallen rubble. Heaving chunks of rock aside, he quickly cleared a pathway. Ruby and Danny landed in the shallow water behind him as a thunderous groan echoed above.

"Run!" Jack cried, then set off as fast as he could, splashing through the cold water. Crashing booms rang out behind them as they followed the passageway, turning a corner and racing up a stairway, finally reaching dry ground. But still the walls shook, and chunks of stone pattered down from the roof.

Only when the thuds and booms had faded to a distant rumble and the ground felt calm once more, did they dare to stop to catch their breath.

"That was way too close," Danny gasped, as he slumped down.

Ruby looked at the ground, her whole body sagging with defeat. "And the Agent escaped!"

Jack's thoughts flicked to Dr Jabari, getting sicker by the day, her skin slowly turning the silver-grey of Xanthrum. He suddenly felt cold, despite the sweat he'd worked up running. But then a thought struck him. Shaking, he touched Ruby's arm, meeting her eyes as she looked up.

"We might not have caught the Agent yet," he told her, "but we do have the second compass piece. I'm certain he'll stop at nothing to get it. And when he comes, we'll be ready..."

THE END

ADAM BLADE

TEAM HERO

THE NIGHT THIEF

MEGA-SELLING
AUTHOR OF
Beast
Quest

READ ON FOR A SNEAK
PEEK AT BOOK 15:

THE NIGHT THIEF

WATER DRIPPED from a crack in the domed ceiling high above. It spattered across the stone mezzanines, bridges and stairs that made up the vast chamber. But what had been a dark and dank ruin was now lit up with floating fluorescent lights, brought in by the archaeologists and other specialists working for Team Hero. They were there to gather intelligence about the lost Taah Lu city, and the Hidden Army who had fought them five thousand years ago.

Jack and his friends watched the specialists work, snapping photos of the elaborate carvings on the walls and measuring the crumbled buildings.

There was particular interest in the strange metallic pieces scattered across the floor near to where Jack and his friends stood — the remains of a soldier of the Hidden Army. Plates and cogs, blades and gears made of silver and gold, all piled up in disarray. Jack shuddered to think what the deadly machine would have looked like when fully assembled.

"I wish Mum could see all this," said Ruby sadly. "She's spent her whole life studying the Taah Lu."

"She'll get better soon," said Danny. "Dr Poe knows what he's doing."

They all turned to where the Team Hero physician was examining Dr Jabari. She looked completely normal but for one thing — the metallic film that coated her eyes. *Xanthrum*. Jack knew little about the exotic substance other than that it was deadly, and that the Agent seemed to have an endless supply. In small doses, it could make a person powerful, but over time could poison you. No one knew how long Dr Jabari had left if they couldn't find a cure.

"Small steps," encouraged Dr Poe. "Your heart rate is high."

Dr Jabari stumbled and collapsed into his arms.

"Mum!" cried Ruby, rushing forwards.

Dr Poe lowered Ruby's mother on to a stretcher.

"It's all right," said Dr Jabari. "I think I just overdid it. Come closer, Ruby." Jack's friend stood by the stretcher and took her mother's hand.

"I'm right here, Mum," she said. Dr Poe was monitoring a tablet with his patient's vital signs, and Jack didn't like the worried frown on his face.

He doesn't know any more about Xanthrum than the rest of us.

Above them, a group of archaeologists were working on a hovering scaffold, recording a large section of the chamber wall that was covered in carvings. Jack had seen enough of the scenes of chaos already. The images showed ranks and ranks of spherical objects bristling with blades, weapons of some sort, sweeping across the land, leaving crumbled towers, flattened trees, and terrified people in their wake. A wave of merciless terror and destruction that eventually wiped the Taah Lu off the face of the earth.

And it'll do the same to us, if we

don't stop the Agent.

Jack's heart felt hollow. They'd triumphed over the Agent twice already, but it looked like those victories meant nothing, if the Chancellor's vision was correct.

"Someone's coming," said Professor Yokata, and her hands fell to the blaster pistols holstered at her hips.

Check out the next book:
THE NIGHT THIEF
to find out what happens next!

IN EVERY BOOK OF
TEAM HERO SERIES
FOUR there is a special
Power Token. Collect
all four tokens to get
an exclusive Team Hero
Club pack. The pack
contains everything you and
your friends need to form your
very own Team Hero Club.

FREE TEAM HERO CLUB PACK

MEMBERSHIP CARDS • MEMBERSHIP CERTIFICATE • STICKERS • POWER GAME • BOOKMARKS

Just fill in the form below, send it in with your four tokens
and we'll send you your Team Hero Club Pack.

SEND TO: Team Hero Club Pack Offer, Hachette Children's Books,
Marketing Department, Carmelite House, 50 Victoria Embankment,
London, EC4Y 0DZ.

CLOSING DATE: 31st December 2019

WWW.TEAMHEROBOOKS.CO.UK

Please complete using capital letters (*UK and Republic of Ireland residents only*)

FIRST NAME

SURNAME

DATE OF BIRTH

ADDRESS LINE 1

ADDRESS LINE 2

ADDRESS LINE 3

POSTCODE

PARENT OR GUARDIAN'S EMAIL

I'd like to receive Team Hero email newsletters and information about
other great Hachette Children's Group offers (I can unsubscribe at any time)

Terms and conditions apply. For full terms and conditions please go to
teamherobooks.co.uk/terms

TEAM HERO Club packs
available while stocks last.
Terms and conditions apply.

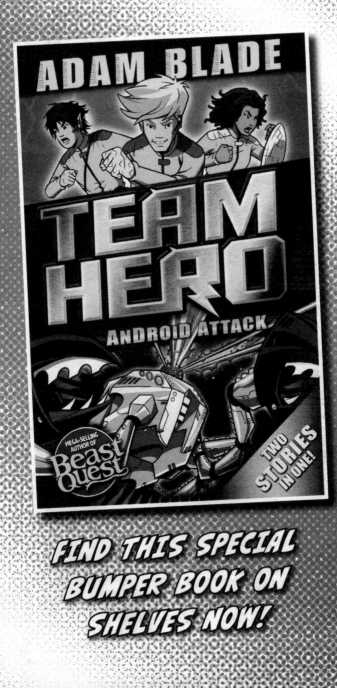

FIND THIS SPECIAL BUMPER BOOK ON SHELVES NOW!

**READ MORE FROM
ADAM BLADE** IN

www.beastquest.co.uk